THE BOOK OF
THE RAVEN-HUNTER.

BENJAMEN GRANT

iUniverse, Inc.
New York   Bloomington

The Book of the Raven-Hunter.

iUniverse books may be ordered through booksellers or by contacting:

iUniverse
1663 Liberty Drive
Bloomington, IN 47403
www.iuniverse.com
1-800-Authors (1-800-288-4677)

ISBN: 978-1-4502-2913-5 (sc)
ISBN: 978-1-4502-2915-9 (ebook)

Printed in the United States of America

iUniverse rev. date: 04/26/2010

PROLOGUE:

"Children, now if you will please turn your pages to 43. Elrich if you could read the above passage for the class." Said a very birdlike humanoid called an avian.

A small grey skinned child with two horns stood up in front of a class of several other grey skinned children with two horns and avian kids. He wore an ordinary school uniform and seemed quite unlike the other children that surrounded him in the room.

"The 41st avian division also known as the gilded axe was the first unit to mix within its ranks the new found brothers of the Necrolytes some millennia ago."

"Very good Elrich now what is the significance of this event?"

A little girl raised her hand so far that it would seem like her arm would come right out of its socket.

"Yes you Rhapsody do you have an idea as to why this is so important?"

"Because," said the little girl very proudly. Because it marked desegregation in the army that would then go into the rest of our world."

"Very good as usual Rhapsody," said the teacher with a smile. "You see children when General Stowe became one of the first Avians to bring about integration in the army all the rest followed along with it. This has created the integrated society to which we all live and thrive

1

now. Now all of you are dismissed for recess I'll see you back here in half an hour's time."

All of the happy children jumped from their seats and streamed towards the doors and out to the school yard. All except for Rhapsody who stayed in her seat reading a large book silently.

"You know Rhapsody you really should go outside and have fun with the other children," said the young avian teacher.

"But I can't learn anything if I'm outside teacher. Besides I like to rest while I have this time."

The teacher got up from her desk and walked slowly to where Rhapsody sat. She looked down on the little girl, while Rhapsody looked up her violet eyes full of shattered innocence.

"You were limping when you came in today. Did something happen to you?"

"I was climbing a tree and a branch broke and I fell down and hurt my leg."

"You said that two weeks ago Rhapsody. About the bruised arms remember?"

"I did. Well I I I." Rhapsody started to cry uncontrollably. "Oh please don't send me away I don't want to be eaten by a kell I don't I don't."

The teacher held her softly in her arms and gently calmed her in the gentle voice only reserved for those who truly feel saddened for the individual.

From outside a window an on looking elrich stared into the window. 'Teachers pet,' was all he said as he turned and walked away.

CHAPTER 1

Times change like the leave that fall from the tree and float to earth

The mud was wet and cold. The swamp was thick with trees so clustered together that the light seemed to barely penetrate. The same could be said about the lofty methane air that seemed to linger almost trapped by the shadowy lofty swamp. A creature that resembled a wolf-like humanoid began walking knee deep in the gooey mud. His skin was wrapped in sheet like metal that covered his torso. He wore a leg-open skirt that had become ruined in the mud as well as a sword that was hoisted on his back.

He scooped his hand into the mud and raised it to his nose. A quick sniff was all he needed to tell.

"Trions have been this way." He said as he began to trudge through the swamp a little faster.

His face brimmed with seriousness and his eyes pointed straightforward in stark determination. Soon he found himself oozing out of the infected wasteland. With his legs now freed he began to break into a jog. From this point the environment seemed to shift suddenly shifted to that of an endless plain that seemed to stretch on for miles of tall grass. Yellow in color like golden and green waves for as far as the eye could see, and oh how the air smelled so much sweeter coming from that thick methane landscape to that of sweet fresh air of wildflowers among the tall grass. The creature began turning his head this way and that trying to catch any scent that seemed to point him in the direction of his laden opponents.

And then it hit. Not one of any Trionic enemy, but that of his own people.

A group of creatures, who stood much in the same way as humans, yet with very wolf-like faces, covered head to toe in fur. The feet were much like dogs, yet their hands were three-fingered claws with a thumb.

He looked in the distance and began to see a group of large objects. As they grew closer he could make out shapes. Little by little they grew into focus until he could see large wolves about the size of cattle come thundering down the plains toward him and before he could think of turning and running the wolves were just a few yards from him.

He took a step back and looked at the wolves. Among these mighty steeds there sat wolf-like humanoids. A few of them had bows pointed at him. At the center sat a well built one who wore a large helmet that covered its entire face. It wore the same armor as the lone warrior without a mount, as well as a long cape which floated in the breeze.

"Raven-Hunter?" The masked one spoke. "How dare you think it to come any where near the tower?"

Raven turned and stared at the masked one eye to eye and spoke gruffly.

"I would no more wish to return to your dominion, than I would to be eaten by the very beasts that stalk the underworld. Know this that I have come hear for good reason and I will part ways with this junction as soon as I'm finished."

"Raven, what possible business could you have to come back?"

"Well, if one could be allowed to speak his words without being torn down, one would appreciate it greatly Blood Scream!"

The bows were pulled back in a way to that would certainly lead to instant death for Raven. A low laugh reverberated through the helmet.

"So it seems, brother. You seem to be doing well. What with your fur long and ragged, your armor rusty. And this was probably the best of clothes that you owned and look at them - tattered and muddy and they smell of a putrid odor. I can only find it fitting that I let you beg for your old life back. Maybe I might be able to allow you to come back and carry around my weapons how does that sound?"

"It's not my life dear sister that I've come to speak of. It's yours and your people. For the Trions navy has dropped a garrison of soldiers. Even now the Trions move upon your borders. They could be attacking the guardians by nightfall tomorrow.

"You think we have not planned for this? The guardians may fall but they will give us good warning."

"Have you ever thought it foolish that you place your entire population into a single fortification?"

"The ancestors built it for a reason; without them we are nothing. They are the way! This is coming from a man who wished to break the most sacred tradition of the stars?"

"This is coming from someone who simply wants to be more than what I was told I could be."

Blood-Scream dismounted from her steed and stepped down to Raven. It was apparent that Scream was much taller than Raven.

"So the runt of the litter thinks he is above the law of the ancestors?" Raven stepped back his position still remained tall. Raven than raised his hand and pulled a sharp blade from the sheath on his back. A low chuckle rumbled from underneath the helmet.

Scream turned back to her steed and drew from one of the large saddle bags a large hammer. She held it in her hand than walked slowly to Raven. The blackness from the helmet pierced Raven. His feet began to tremble but he didn't back down.

"Do you know what strife you brought upon yourself?" Scream said as she swung the large hammer from her side. Raven Ducked and rolled out of its reach. He than slashed his sword at her ankle. And with a lurch the large kell stumbled, then hopped and began to growl a guttural sound of anger.

"Your moves have become predictable sister."

"You think that you can kill me, then?"

"That was never my intention dear sister, but if you will not listen to reason, then I will leave you to die and find another way to defend my home."

"Wait," Scream stumbled over to Raven.

"You have beaten me. And for that the ancient law demands that your request be heard. I will take you to the main tower after we take a trip to one of the guardians."

Ears twinge forward as Raven's face turned to that of curiosity.

"Has it been so long you begin to forget our ways brother?" Raven turned and walked toward the steed, sheathing his sword as he did.

Scream stumbled behind him and placed the large mallet in the bag, and was helped onto her wolf.

And with a great howl they began to ride through the plains until they came upon a great ten story tower. Its foundation was that of great stones that seemed that they would not budge even during the strain of a great earthquake. It was held fastened and even by a great number of long large chains that stretched down to the earth.

As they rode, Raven began to feel a chill run down his spine. Oh to be back again after eleven years.

CHAPTER 2: BACK INTO THE WORLD

Some races search their entire life for purpose. Meanwhile the stars tell us ours, and for that reason is it not safe to say that we are the most advanced of all races?

-Kell philosopher

"MEDIC!!!" The shouts and yells made from Scream echoes throughout the whole of the old tower. Warriors from all over scrambled to find any medical operatives to help their proud commander find some attention to the flesh wounds that ached her angered her spirit and choked at her pride. And it was in this screaming and yelling that Raven was able to duck into the base level of the tower. He moved through the doors and he slowly walked about the large room. An odd sense of nostalgia gripped him as he moved to what seemed to be a large stable where giant wolves that serve as steeds to the kell forces sat and slumbered. They were all humped together and sleeping on one another. These now gentle creatures were the heart of the kell army themselves they had allowed so many times for them to rush into the heart of the fray. As he walked Raven reminisced of older days; of those old times that he had to ride into carnage and death. The wolves seemed very peaceful now; much more so than they have been then the last time he saw them.

As he walked to on looking for that special wolf he found a scraggly

7

old looking wolf not sleeping with the group but rather off in the corner. His fur was black and his eyes were yellow much the same way as raven. Both had scars from ages past, as well as scruffy hair that looked matted.

"We once were as close as a man and his dog could get weren't we boy?" Raven said stroking the mane of the once proud wolf. "We've both seen better days haven't we?"

There was a yelp from the dog that signified a yes. And Raven began to stroke the back of his friend. And then with a shock he realized that he could feel the bones of the old wolf.

"You haven't been eating well, have you?" Raven said feeling his eyes watering up. "The pack must have ostracized you, haven't they. I'm so sorry old boy; I tried as hard as I could to take you with me, but I was barely able to make it out alive on my own. Raven rested his head against his wolf friend and the tears of his past began to trickle out like the sands of time. "I have to leave now, but I won't leave you stranded for far too long, okay?"

Doors began to creak open, knowing that the other members of the tower would not like that he had injured the leader he knew his only way to try and come out of this was to run so He ran up a flight of stairs fast as he could go. He ran up to the second floor which was lined with living quarters all the way across the hall. And it was at the end of that hallway there stood a figure very familiar to Raven.

"I guess my sources are correct," said the mysterious figure from down the hall. Raven stared directly at that figure who was wearing a black cloak that concealed his entire body. As the figure grew closer a snout could be seen protruding from the head of the cloak. It was wolf-like; as the kell drew closer Raven could almost sense an aura of power coming from the figure as he drew closer to Raven with every step.

"Master?" Raven asked, mouth gaping … "after all this time? Why are you here?"

"The question is why did you return, Raven-Hunter?"

"Master, please - Trions are on the move with the means to destroy this beloved land."

"You've seen the Trions then with your own eyes?"

"You know me well master, would I fabricate this?"

The dusk came shining through, and the old master face was revealed. It was young and fresh like a cub who had just become an adult.

"Master I think you would be the only one to believe me."

"Yes to help those that you love you have sacrificed much, and gained very little, Raven I hope you know that you have my sympathy. I shall believe you. Though the hard part will be to make others see the way you do, but I shall do my best."

"Thank you. I know your power over the Tower leader is like law."

"Right. I must hurry so that they will have time to plot proper defenses." The young looking Kell looked at his pupil "We shall meet again - of this I am sure."

And in a flash of fire the master disappeared from the student as quickly as he came.

"How could a person just be able to fade into nothingness? He's more powerful than I ever expected."

Raven took a step forward. "He truly is a champion isn't he?"

Suddenly Raven felt the odd sensation of a poke of a spear at his back, "You really thought we'd let someone like you just walk around this place without being able to keep an eye on you?" spoke a very thuggish looking kell. Raven raised his arms and a rope was tied around them.

He was then led to a basement floor where he was put into a dank dark cell.

From there all his clothing was stripped, and the cold enveloped him. He was in a dark, wet, maggot infested cell, but as least he was alone.

Or so he thought.

"You know friend," came a very raspy sounding voice. "I don't see much company these days."

"Same here, but up until a little while ago it was my choice."

"Oh?" The voice seemed to inch close than stopped.

"These bars seem to hold me in. Though it seem less than those chains that tie you down."

"Hmm and how would you know of this stranger? I seem pretty blind in these halls."

"One's sight does improve as time goes on." The raspy voice laughed, "And time is all that I have now."

Raven turned toward the sound of the voice.

"For what reason did they lock you in this cell?" Raven asked

"Well the reasons are many but first and foremost is that I am a Necrolyte."

"You mean the Dark Users?"

"Some call us by that name."

"But isn't it true that your people engage frequently in the dark arts of the netherworlds?"

"Yes. Much in the way your people engage in earth and fire magic."

"You're infused with those powers?"

"Yes we will forever be cursed by the mistakes of those who came before us."

"But I am told we draw the abilities of such magic from our ancestors."

"This is true that souls gather around us and allow us to use their magic. But we are a little different than you Kells.

"Well in what way?" questioned Raven.

"Our abilities cause nothing but pain. They are only able to serve that purpose."

"Yet how does that have anything to do with your ancestors?"

"Because a long millennia ago they took this magic, willingly. They fully knew that with any magic there's always the desire to use it."

"Yes, a certain lust does seem to consume some people, that is if they are unable to control it and then end up getting lost inside of it. I mean they just keep on using and using and then next thing you know they're consumed with it.

"Yes, well quite the opposite can happen."

"Well how so?" Raven asked.

"If you stop…" the raspy voice grew on "you can only take it to a point, and than a binge happens."

Raven instinctively took two steps away from the voice.

"I'm sorry to startle you. Maybe if I could explain exactly my reasons. Then things will become clear."

CHAPTER 3: THE PRISONER'S TALE

What are we without our sins? Our faults? For it does seem that in my time I have seen these two things truly create are deepest character and show who we truly are.

-Rose (Trion Senator)

"First of all I think you should know my name; names are after all just a teensy bit important." came the raspy sounding voice. "I am Rhapsody. And who are you?"

"I once called myself Raven-Hunter. Though now that name means little to me."

"Well then I'll combine the two together. Then it could mean something. Lets see what if we just shorten it down to Raven? Now I think that's much finer name than that long word Raven-Hunter?"

"To be honest Rhapsody, I think it sucks," said Raven.

"Well why do you really like having the hunter added to it? Gees, it's just a name and it could give you a whole new lease on life."

"Yeah and you know what my life has been going well so far I mean by the stars just look at this sitting in a cage naked, oh boy always wanted this to happen." There was a raspy laugh that echoed throughout the cell.

"Well if you don't want to, fine. But you're the one with such a negative attitude. I mean crystal seriously all I did was give you a suggestion and boom you blow it off. Besides I'm sure you haven't had it that bad. Well at least I think it can't be any harsher than what I've gone through."

"And what the hell did you go through that was so bad?"

"Oh yeah! Now let me see where exactly should I begin on telling you this?"

"You do know that the beginning is sometimes accepted as the easiest place to start."

"Okay then," Rhapsody replied. "I guess I should tell you first off that I never wanted to learn that sick art. I was forced to. My parents you see, they believed highly in the military. I was told that was the only way to become a good member of society."

"I take it your parents were military people?" Raven asked.

"More than that," grimaced Rhapsody "They were sadists. They saw this curse as a gift they should use to protect their lands. Yet they enjoyed their jobs too much. They took to using it on the enemy, each other and me."

Raven stood up and began to walk over to Rhapsody's voice.

"I'm sorry Rhapsody. I had no idea."

"It's okay," Rhapsody whispered "The point is, from that I wanted nothing more than just to please them, so they would stop using me as a target."

"So you joined with them to try and stop the abuse."

"Pretty much, but you see it merely let me open up to become them. Once I opened my gate and began to gather the souls around me, I would always feel twisted or shattered or just more plainly cursed."

"So you never used it. The dark magic I mean?"

"I had to - once you're in, it's off you go. Pretty much though, I never used it unless I was forced. But that proved to have dire consequences."

"Did you lose control?"

"Yeah," Rhapsody began to sob. "I blacked out and then when I came to." There was a pause as the sobbing grew more intense. "I had killed my family. Everyone my parents, my sibling....my partner a...a...a... and my child. My tiny son. I was banished after that. Forced to journey, I managed to move away from the great forests of Tarlik Guarde all the way down to these plains. There, this female kell attacked me and sent me into a whirlwind of feelings. In the panic I used the magic again and permanently scarred her face. But then I found myself in here. And for awhile I was alone. And in that darkness I used the magic on myself to keep me in check. To hide the fact I truly am a monster, cursed with powers I can't control. Too weak to control it." The sobbing seemed to dry up a little and Raven sat there with nothing that he felt he could say. Finally he spoke slowly, calmly and deliberately.

"The spirits have been cruel to you thus far," there was a pause so he could collect himself. "But what if I help you make it better?"

"How can you? A beast will always be a beast."

"Yet every beast has a heart and you are no different. You just need a little help along the way. Some kind of friend that can help you.

"Why would you do this?"

"Because it won't be right to escape and leave someone as nice as you behind."

"How do you plan on escaping from here? All these Kells guarding all around this area. And they never come close to where we are not even in meal times," Criticized Rhapsody.

"Oh you don't know my sister. Scream will come to gloat at just the right moment."

"And you have some big plan for this grand escape?"

"In fact Rhapsody I do," spoke Raven very matter of fact like. Raven walked as close to the voice as the chain would let him. "And listen close because I hate repeating myself."

CHAPTER 4: FROM THE ASHES

Light shined through on the two's dark and dusty prison. The door swung open and with a thud there stood a large Kell standing in the door way.

"Well, Raven - how have the past two weeks been on my little brother? Are you comfy?"

"How about you come and talk like a normal person eh scream? The shadows might do you some good."

She began to walk over blindly, stepping on various items that stood in her way. Hearing the clang Raven noticed something odd about it. Not flesh against metal. But metal against metal. She was wearing a complete set of armor, complete with her giant hammer. It was a square shaped piece of iron, with a long handle that seemed almost as long as the kell herself.

Raven was choked from the darkness. Then he was thrown from it. The chains that held him down snapped and Raven flew across the room landing with a thud against the cage.

"Raven," Rhapsody screamed.

Scream began to move toward the cage swiftly with hammer in hand. But then she suddenly stopped. She dropped the hammer with a thud, and began to breathe heavily.

"I can't...feel...my...chest." Scream fell to the ground and began to pant out of control.

"This isn't your day is it?" Raven said standing down upon his sister. "You know?" he said with a frown. You're not half as good as you think you are." Then he shot a fire ball. "Rhapsody get out of the way of the cage." The orb hit with a thud and an explosion rang out throughout the tower. "Rhapsody, come on" Raven turned toward the exit swinging his chain and smashed down the guard. Then he turned back to face Rhapsody viewing his friend for the first time in the light. The creature that was in front of him was tall and pale. Two horns jutted from her head, and curved upward a little bit. They weren't too large but still quite visible. Her hair was long and black, and she had a broad pretty smile across her face, which almost seemed surreal, matched with the many scars that seemed to be all across her body. She had rags of clothing that seemed to barely cling to her skinny form. Her eyes were beautiful; they seemed to be of the deepest shade of lavender that almost seemed to be a royal purple.

Raven stood awestruck for a moment. Rhapsody stared back for a moment. Then she turned and her face became serious.

"If the trions are here, then we need to hurry. We don't know how much time we have."

"Well the army is close, you can see the riders from the window - they are in full charge toward the enemy. So that means its just begun.

Then a great booming sound erupted, followed by a loud crash.

"Artillery fire?" asked Rhapsody

"Yeah but it was definitely the trions doing the firing."

"So if we don't hurry we could end up in another prison?" Rhapsody turned toward the stairs "Like hell Raven - I'm not being forced into another cage."

She ran head long down the stairs with Raven following after her.

"We need to avoid the third floor."

"Got it but aren't we on the first floor?"

"No prison should be at the top. That way we can't exactly escape in a hurry." Replied Raven.

The downward staircase seemed to prove Raven correct and he gave her a smug look.

"We need to get to the fourth floor first. That's the armory, and then we need to head to the first. But we could chain ride down there."

"Chain ride?" asked Rhapsody.

"Yeah - use the chains that help keep the tower on base and use that to slide down to the bottom. All the warriors are taught how to do this.

"But our eyes haven't fully adjusted yet," Insisted Rhapsody.

"There's no time, just hold on to the rail of the stairs for all you got."

They started down clumsily and slowly at first but gradually picked up speed. They got to the fourth and they could see that the battle was in full motion. The Trions' cannons seemed to be holding the charging kells at bay.

"Damn, I was expecting more to be here." Raven as they walked into the almost bare room.

And it appeared that the room once contained vast amounts of weapons, but had since been cleared due to the battle that was going on outside.

Rhapsody looked about and picked up a diamond shape shield.

"Well this one seems quite nice, and it's something that hardly seems deadly."

"But is that the point Rhapsody?"

"You never know Raven, you never know."

Raven turned back to his search. He looked through the bramble of weapons; he became frustrated though, as he couldn't find the one weapon that he had been searching for.

"Dammit they don't have one. What the hell are we supposed to do?"

"Calm down." Rhapsody gently spoke as she walked over to him and gently patted his back. "So you don't have what you want - just find a way to make do without it."

Raven sat and looked at the pile for a while, then with a shrug he picked up the first sword he saw.

"I won't like this one you know."

"Well you don't have to Raven, but we do have to get out of here, now don't we?"

Rhapsody turned and headed towards the door. Raven swung the sword a few times, and then followed Rhapsody.

"Now explain how we ride these chains?"

Raven looked out, grasped the chain, then looked at Rhapsody.

"Climb on my back and hold on tight. I'm going to climb down it." She jumped on his back and grabbed on by the great amounts of fur he had. Once she was on securely, Raven began to descend down.

With a thud they both landed on the soft grass.

"Raven?" Rhapsody said staggering around then puking all over the grass. "Please don't do that again." Raven would have laughed, but the battle seemed to take full stage with swords clanging and explosions every which way. Raven broke into a sprint with Rhapsody behind towards the tower.

Kells moved past him as they came in a mighty charge. So much so they failed to notice that above them were giant Rays beginning to swoop down upon them. Crashes and explosions rang out on all side and with a shock Raven realized that the trions had brought a full army and it was now pointed to bear on the unsuccessful guard. Raven came to the tower door and burst it open with such force he nearly cracked the door down. Standing between him and the steed he needed to ride, was his older sister Scream.

"You think you have won dear brother?" There was laughing from underneath that soulless helmet, her hammer cocked back ready to strike. "Well I'm still here and that means you lose, doesn't it you weakling?"

She came charging full speed and the ground rose, forming a tunnel for no escape except through her.

She was ten feet away. Raven held both hands onto his sword. Nine feet away. Raven started to chant.

"erif ekam yom edabb gnorts htiw erif daen tseh.. Seven feet away. His blade began to glow red hot. Three feet away. Scream began to bring the hammer down with such force that energy was erupting from it.

SMASH!!!!!!

The sword and hammer clashed with such ferocity that the raised earth began to shatter and energy was flying every which way.

"YOU BLOOD TRAITOR!!!!!!"

Scream shouted.

"YOU VILE KILLER!!!!!"

Raven shouted back. And the hate that fueled their souls was enough that a crack in the earth was forming under them. And a raging fire around them. Raven felt the crack drawing closer. He lost grip of the sword and knew that he was the weaker half in this duel. And just as he did he felt himself being pulled away slowly. But it was not a huge shove just enough to dodge the hammer as it came down upon the ground and became jammed tightly into the crevice.

Raven looked and saw a very pale grey arm thrusting a diamond shaped shield into the former owner of that hammer. And he watched as it came under the soulless metal and pierced the neck of his most hated sibling. And with a startle he realized it to be no dream or fantasy.

"Rhapsody?" he turned and shouted, and all at once the fold of reality caught up with him again.

He fell to the ground, Rhapsody coming to lift him up ... Scream's body being flung backwards, and landing with a thud.

"Raven are you okay?" Rhapsody asked fearfully. "Raven come on buddy - speak to me."

"We need to get that black wolf," Raven was trying to croak out.

"Okay you mean the one farthest down?"

"Yes take the tie around him off. Then he should understand what to do."

"Alright I'll go do it. You think you'll be okay?"

"Yeah fine as a feather," and that was all he could say as the blackness enveloped him and he past out.

CHAPTER 5: FREEDOM?

Under the cerulean skies doth the trion council lie.

The air was sweet, the breeze seemed like such a relief from the cold dampness of their former prison. The grass felt soft and nice as Raven, coming out of a great sleep.

"We're by a lake, aren't we?" Raven asked as he opened his eyes.

"You are - but that's not quite the point, is it?" said a voice that seemed familiar and yet not.

Raven jolted up and began to look this way and that.

"What's the matter?" asked the same voice.

"Who is it? he asked curiously.

"Someone who helped you break out of jail."

Raven perked up and saw out bathing in the lake a grey feminine figure. Her skin now clean one could easily see many great and hideous scars that streaked across her body. Her hair long and black now seemed to fall all the way down to her butt now that she could straighten it as she ran her fingers through it. As she came walking back to him he could see that scars seemed to be everywhere on her body except her face. To which was rounded with a pretty nose; she had full lips, a broad smile ... and two small horns that jutted from her forehead almost seemed to add to the whole image of beauty. But the thing that he hadn't noticed until then was her big innocent looking purple eye. That seemed to almost hold all of her grace.

She gracefully stepped from out of the water and sat beside him.

"We barely got out of there, you know." Rhapsody's broad smile revealed a number of sharp looking white teeth.

"Did I miss it all?"

"Well nearly. But then again you put all your soul behind trying to take down Scream. If you think about it, it's a bit of a miracle you're alive."

"That's true. You did save me back there with that shield."

"No I think we worked more as a team," she said "The important thing is that we got out before that tower collapsed."

"NO!!" Raven shouted "what happened to make it collapse?"

"Well I think it was you and Scream going all out like you did. It kinda shook the foundation a bit."

"Really? I didn't think that could happen."

Raven got up and looked around

"So I take it that you just jumped on the wolf and he fled?"

"Yeah the little beast went off chasing a deer a while ago why?"

"Well it seems like he might have just caught his old riders scent and went to see him."

"Wait you mean you don't have a steed?"

"Well Rhapsody," he paused for a moment, "He died a while ago. He was stabbed by an enemy."

Rhapsody stood up and began to walk over to a pile that was sitting on the ground.

"You know you're lucky that wolf had clothes in the saddle bag I stole because I'm not staring at your bum as we go wherever it is that you live."

"What," Raven stood there aghast for a moment, "you know you're one to talk - I mean look at you."

"What about me; what's so wrong with me?" Rhapsody asked incredulously.

"Theres nothing wrong with how you look; its just I think you should wear at least something for where were going."

With her arms crossed she handed Raven the article of clothing without looking, saying "alright".

They dressed and began to walk towards the forest, not saying a word as they passed the huge trees and listened to the sounds of various birds. At last they reached a little house carved right into the side of a tree, and what seemed like a little grey old kell standing outside. His hair seemed to be growing in odd tufts with various patches missing. He was playing with the black wolf that had been his steed so many years ago.

"Father, I'm back."

Raven began to walk faster and than burst into a run hands outstretched waiting for a hug and then, BAM!!!! Raven was smacked in the face by his father's cane.

"You little hooligan how many times have I told you not to bring strangers home with you? And I swear this one looks pretty strange now doesn't she my boy?"

"Well I'm sorry dad but you see me..." BAM!!! Another whack from the cane.

"You lost my armor and sword. Seriously now what happened out there? Did your big sister pick on you? Cause if she did you have to be the bigger man and not fight back. You know that my boy. And I'm not even a main warrior."

"He didn't have much of a choice," spoke up Rhapsody.

"You, you are a necrolyte, aren't you girl?" questioned the old kell.

"Why yes I am, my name is Rhapsody and what is yours?"

He walked slowly with his cane, Rhapsody walked as well keeping so that the two would keep eye contact with each other. Then she moved forward to greet him. He looked her up and down then turned toward Raven then to her, and back again.

"You found this girl trapped on the trip didn't you?"

"Yes Father."

"Well dear, my name is Star Seeker though most just call me Seeker. Except for this annoying one over there - he just calls me dad" He smiled and offered a hand to be shook. He was considerable smaller than Rhapsody so she had to bend over slightly so she could shake it. "Would you kindly come in … oh, and be careful of the door."

They walked into a cozy little house with star charts and other astronomy equipment lying all around the little room that made up the living room.

They moved into what seemed like a small kitchen with a table being part of the tree and a little fire place where a pot of stew was cooking.

"I'm sorry for all the clutter," he spoke "Its just that I'm finally going to get a breakthrough on this research I've been doing. This way now to sit down.

"Nothing like a big pot of stew waiting for you for when you get back, now isn't there?"

"You know how much I love it," Raven said sarcastically

They knelt and Seeker turned to Raven, scooping out some stew.

"You know I'm quite proud of you." Raven seemed to bow in gratitude.

"Thank you sir."

"But it would seem that things are all for naught," Seeker said sadly.

"How so Grandpa? Have you grown ill?"

"No but my research has proved only the opposite of what I wanted."

"What research?" asked Rhapsody.

"Well my young dear" Seeker said clearing his throat "You know the belief system that kells entire lives are determined by the language of the stars?"

"Yeah I heard a little. But I always thought it was just referring to their occupation? Does it decide more than that?"

"Well you see I wanted to break that idea. Prove the ancients were wrong with the occupation thing. But most of the research that I have done has in fact proven quite the opposite. Its like the language has been done and done so many times and left room to fix glaring errors that there's been in that the language itself is nearly perfect. I mean the whole thing is charted and done. I mean honestly to this date I've only found one person that seems to break the mold and he stands with us this very evening enjoying the best damn soup he's ever tasted."

"So in short because my father wanted to figure out why the way it was he ended up doing research that the leaders didn't like and so it ended up in the both of us being banished. Well I was already going to be banished because I could never really get into the whole killing for no reason. I would have much better enjoyed just to sit around and be able to write some poetry."

"That seems kinda stupid I mean why can't they just go over the law of the ancients."

Both Raven and Seeker looked at her with the most incredulous look.

"Well I mean honestly - can't they change them now ... to correct the mistake that was made earlier by them?"

"But Rhapsody," spoke Seeker. "They made sure that the system is so flexible that it is close to perfect and very rarely does anyone break the mold. So much so that most just don't care about trying to change it anymore."

"So they just let go of the both of you? Instead of trying to fix a mistake and maybe correct the x-factors?"

"Yeah we can never return to our homes again," spoke Seeker.

"That is really sad, and stupid."

"Oh its nothing to fret about my dear now you just tell me a little bit about yourself."

CHAPTER 6: THE DATE.

Kells do not have a system of marriage. Rather they have a system that states that joint property value should be measure by how long the two partners have lived together. This means in essence that physical goods become more jointed whether they be living with a friend or lover. The Kells also do not find a differential between gay or straight nor love romance or long term friendships.

Raven readied his make shift bow and surveyed the forest floor. He stood upon a tree that overlooked a small patch of mushrooms. These were the perfect hunting spots to find large amounts of deer. The sun was shooting up from behind mountains that faced them. The due was shining on the ground and a mist hung giving it an oddly eerie yet beautiful sight to behold. This was the perfect weather for hunting and raven knew it. From out of the thick of the woods emerged a powerful looking deer that seemed to move with such elegance one could mistake it for a prince. Raven readied the bow and took aim.

"Psst Raven, what are you doing?" a familiar voice said. Raven shot the arrow and it landed on the ground with a thud. And the deer hearing this ran off into the early morning. Raven lay the bow down and looked down to the root of the tree. There standing beside it was Rhapsody. "How's it going Raven?"

"It's going fine. I was just caught a little off guard that's all." Raven forced a smile and waved down to Rhapsody, followed by grumbling incoherently to himself.

"Do you want some help?" asked Rhapsody.

"Sure," said Raven looking down at the beautiful Necrolyte. "Come on up here."

"Thanks I hope I didn't make you mad just then?" Rhapsody asked.

"No not at all," Raven said sarcastically. "Right now though I'm hunting for some food, see out here we have a very limited amount of salt to work with so were forced to have to hunt quite a bit since we have next to no storage for the damn things."

"So that's why every three or four days you're out so early in the morning," Rhapsody said.

"Yea, dad is far too old to do any sort of hunting. But he does like to cook. So I let him do that even though its god awful. Personally I don't see how you haven't said anything about it."

"Well I don't really think it's that bad. Besides you guys have taken me in. I don't know if I should be making too many complaints."

"It's okay. I know that I would never kick out someone as pretty as you."

"Well it's always good to know you keep me around so I can stand around and look pretty." Rhapsody said smiling.

Raven blushed and cleared his throat. "I didn't mean it like that. I was just trying to give you a compliment."

"I know. Don't worry I find it very flattering."

"Oh I guess I just don't know quite how to woo people. I've never been that great when it comes to people that I well." Raven stopped nervousness gripping him like a thorn bush.

"That you what Raven? That you enjoy that I came with you when we freed ourselves from that prison?"

"Yes that's what I mean. You're a really good friend Rhapsody and you mean a lot to me."

"You mean a lot to me too Raven, I think more than you know."

He smiled as he looked into her violet eyes. It stood interlocked with his yellow eyes for a time. And in that moment it seemed almost like there was nothing around them. They slowly moved closer together. Their lips touched and in an instant they kissed. Raven shut his eyes and it felt as if waves of warm melted butter were flowing through his veins. They backed away, each one dazed by the moment that had just hit the both of them.

"Wow," said Raven smiling. "I haven't felt quite like that in years."

"Really," said Rhapsody. "To be honest I've only ever have had one partner in love. And even with that person we never consummated."

Raven looked out towards the trees. It was now well into the morning with the light shining through the trees and streaming through various parts of the forest.

"Have you ever consummated with someone Raven?" Rhapsody queried.

Raven smiled for a moment then turned his attention to the forest.

"If you don't mind Rhapsody," Raven said very preciously. "I'd rather not discuss things of this nature right now. It's not something that I'm that comfortable with."

"Well its something that you'll be willing to share with me at some point right?"

Raven raised his bow and shot it. It stuck onto a deer that was walking up to the mushroom circle.

"Yea at some point I will tell you anything that you ask me Rhapsody. Just don't be alarmed by the answers you might receive."

She smiled at him as he jumped out of the tree.

"That's okay Raven I can wait."

CHAPTER: 7 POWER

Law 1: A Kells area of profession is chosen. This is general enough as to show a group of many careers that exist inside the slotted profession.

Law 2: A kell is only limited by how hard a kell wants to work the difference between a small time worker and someone who leads the profession is all dependant on how hard a kell wants to work for it.

Law 3: The laws of the ancients are the final law in the area of profession. Anyone who doesn't abide by them or changes what the stars say so that they can fit their own means will be punished.

SO SAYS THE ANCIENTS

The forest of Dark whisper is by far an eerie place to the rest of the shadowy earth. It is roughly the size of a European country. The trees grow in such a way that they have a great canopy that overshadows the entire under wood of forest and leaves it with little light and consumed in shadow. Though it is lighted by bugs that glow constantly, going around providing a little more light on a forest permanently trapped in twilight.

Among the trees was a tall Necrolyte whose skin is a darkish grey and whose horns seemed to resemble great rams' horns. He walked among the many intertwining branches so naturally that you would think that he was simply walking down the street. Behind him was a birdlike creature covered in brownish grey feathers. His talons seem to just grip the side of the tree so he had no need to weave among the many branches.

"You wonder why we're being called by the matriarch?" the Necrolyte asked.

"I don't know, Elrich. Though you know they may be looking for a great man like me to take over, seeing as how the czar has died an' all. Maybe they realize they need someone who's actually good to do the job for them." The bird-like humanoid began to laugh hysterically like he was a comedic genius. Elrich turned to face him and the laughter immediately stopped and with such stoic seriousness Elrich looked into the birds eyes.

"Cassanova, you should not laugh at one who's dead, for I can show you the pain of death, plus be able to add to it tenfold."

Cassanova straightened up with nothing but fear in his eyes.

"Now," Elrich said coldly "We need to find out what the Matriarch wants us to do."

The two jumped from the tree to tree very quietly as they approached a grand palace that was built into a tree that was as massive as a skyscraper. The tree itself was the color of pure ivory. And the mansion almost seemed to have a glittering effect as it was in the shadows. The highly decorated doors were covered in vines and the place was built with what seemed like marble. Inside the door sat a pretty young necrolyte behind a desk writing away at some document.

"Hey there, you pretty little thing," Cassanova said bringing his beak in as far as he could "How about you give a real man a peck on the beak eh?"

The young girl jerked back and did her best to get out of her chair but soon Cassanova was on top of the desk pulling himself closer to the young girl.

"Well Cassanova," said Elrich looking at the girl in disgust, "You have your fun but as for me, I'm going to see the Matriarch to see what she wants."

Elrich walked down the marble hallway. As he did Cassanova got down from on top of the girl and began to trail along.

"Oh come on man – you're such a buzz kill." Cassanova shouted as he ran after Elrich.

"You play around to much Cassanova it will prove to be your downfall."

"Yeah but never when I'm fighting."

"But even then you're nowhere near as good as the person who has trained you."

"Yeah but I'm trying to get there - I just need some time to catch up that's all."

"But at the same time your master improves."

"But look where that's got us. We're considered like one level below the ten black blades; you know, sent in only to finish the job. End a battle, you know what I'm saying."

They reached the grand room with two great staircases each going in opposite directions that led to two thrones. The one on the right was empty. And on the one on the left there sat an old necrolyte woman who's horns were small and looked as if they had been filed down. Her clothes were that of something that seemed like a kimono. She was adorned with a great headdress made of wood and feathers.

The advisors wore long white hooded robes and each on came up and down shouting orders to nearby guards, who ran among the foreground where Elrich and Cassanova stood.

Then the great elder necrolyte stood up and with a booming cry shouted,

"Step forth oh great warriors."

Cassanova and Elrich stepped forward. There, the advisors quickly flocked to them sweeping to the top of the grand staircase. The Matriarch sat and looked at the two men, from how skinny and emotionless the cloak-wearing Elrich seemed to the bulging bodybuilder with armor and weapons that was Cassanova.

"So the avian," she said pointing to the bird man. "What would your name be?"

"Cassanova," he said grinning

"And you?" the elder woman said.

"I am Elrich," said the necrolyte coolly.

"You two don't seem to match your descriptions, but there is a presence about you."

Cassanova smiled, smugly patting his feathery muscles. The old Necrolyte seemed to stare back and forth between the two as if trying to scope out the true strength.

"Things have become quite unbalanced as of late. With the Avion Czar dead, it leaves all the power to me, the Matriarch." Cassanova began to rub his hands together, while Elrich stood there, his eyes black as night.

"As such a mission like this must be carried out in absolute secrecy. If anyone was to know that I used this time to carry out secret missions I could face execution."

"So that means take out anyone who could stand in our way?" Cassanova asked.

"I don't want any loose ends, you got that?" the Matriarch spoke waving a finger at the two of them.

"Sounds simple enough," said Elrich

"And fun," responded Cassanova. The Matriarch cracked what seemed to be a small smile.

"Good," she said "I have some items to give you just for this mission"

Two of the robed advisors came up, each one carrying a black case.

"To you Cassanova I give you this." One of the robed men said as he opened his box. "It is Shenpo armor. It's made from the finest of metals from our thrones."

Cassanova gripped it in his hand, awestruck.

"I love it" was all he could muster to get out. He then put it into a crate and took it "Which way to the dressing room?" he strutted down the steps and away with pride.

"I wanted to speak with you in private anyway,"

The Matriarch pointed her finger directly at Elrich. "You are the most powerful user of the Necromatic gifts? Is this correct?"

"That I am."

"Are you not considered the most dangerous as well?"

"I wouldn't know."

"Can I trust you?"

"I wouldn't know my queen; only you would."

She stared for a moment carefully considering the response that was put in front of her. "Then I'll give you this sword," she said, and the white robed man opened the box to reveal a black handle.

"This sword is a black dracon blade. It was used during the time of the first dynasty."

Elrich took the blade, examining it with thorough precision.

"This lacks a blade. How am I to fight with it?"

"The blade will form as it is needed. And will form to the energy around you."

A blade suddenly shot from the handle. Curved like a dog's leg and was jet black in color.

"How interesting, so anything I want it to be it will become?"

"Precisely," said the Matriarch "Now when that fool of an apprentice of yours returns we will discuss our battle plan."

CHAPTER 8: THE GIRL

If this world would be darkness let not it consume thee. For thou is like an angel in every degree. And forlorn is that swan then lest to let her be free from a sad and ugly raven like me.

-Raven Hunter

The sun was bright and the sky was a cloudless blue sky. Raven walked across the plains sniffing the air. A big rock would serve as a good resting place, he thought.

He sat letting the sun soak into his dark brown fur. Then closing his eyes and felt himself drift into that oh so familiar dream state.

When he awoke Rhapsody was nestled beside him asleep. She had since found old clothes that seemed to fit. Today it was a white blouse that cut off at her midriff. And white pants that seemed to have grass stains around the ankles. He moved her hair from her face and examined her beautiful face.

"Oh to the ancients there is no such beauty such as she and to think that she would be with a raven such as thee."

He held her soft silver hand and looked up and down her arm. Scars seem to line it readily and his heart seemed to cry out with pain at the site of every one of them.

"Why would anyone scar an angel like she, I should pity them for they are fools and do not know how to appreciate what is truly great in this world. Her eyes began to open and Raven couldn't help but smile.

"Morning Raven," she whispered. She yawned and all her sharp white teeth were exposed. "See I found you sleeping out here and I came up to see if you wanted company. That is if you want me, cause if not I could just leave," she said.

"No you're not intruding, Rhapsody," he said with a smile. "Things have been nice this past week, don't you agree?"

"Yeah I would have to agree with you there," she said snuggling closer to him. "Even though your father likes to ramble on and on about the stars, doesn't he?"

"Yeah," said Raven "But he can't exactly help it. It's what he was born to do."

"Still, I say that's stupid kicking you out for a reason like that." muttered Rhapsody.

"Well they feel really strongly about it." Raven looked away from her to the sky. "Look to the right and you'll see the sunset."

They both turned and looked. The shine of pinks and reds and yellows patched on to a sky blue canvas, then sprinkled here and there with dashes of white clouds. And off in the distance was the shadow of a tower.

"Its beautiful isn't it? The sunset I mean."

Rhapsody said as she looked at him.

"Yeah but you know I can name one thing I know that is ten times prettier than that sunset."

Rhapsody turned and looked at him with a wide grin on her face.

"You really mean that? Or are you saying that just because I'm the only girl around this place?"

"Yes I mean it my dear Rhapsody." Said Raven

Rhapsody started to blush.

"You still miss home don't you?" Rhapsody asked.

"No," said Raven quickly "It's just I think of all those I've hurt by doing this. I mean friends, family, and the people they know are being hurt by that. Cause you know it honestly has to kill dad not to be able to see his wife or his kids, but he always said that he would stand by me during this time. It was like he still feels like he can fix everything, you know. And then everything can all be happy and the way it used to be."

"You know something," Rhapsody said. "You beat yourself up way to much over this sort of thing."

"You think so?" asked Raven.

"Raven I know so," Rhapsody said turning to face him "I mean so many things are at your fingertips and you let them slip by. Poof they're gone, and you're left feeling sorry for yourself. Which I mean on one hand is good for poetry. But you know just as much about sorrow has been written on joy. You shouldn't be dwelling on what you have had taken from you and pain you caused others and think to how you can use that to help better yourself now."

"Hmm, try living a little more happy you say. Go out and just take things that I want, right?"

"Yeah, when you see an opportunity just take it; don't let it pass you by as you sit there."

"You know that does sound pretty good. But there would be a problem - I mean then my name would not fit as well, would it."

"Oh shut up you fool," she said pretending to slap him.

Suddenly Rhapsody jerked up and shook raven by the shoulder and pointed out toward the sky.

"Did you see that little girl, she said pointing in front of her.

Raven stared for a moment before his eyes could concentrate, then he saw it - what looked like a little necrolyte walking around screaming. Rhapsody bolted up and began to chase toward the little girl with Raven right on her tail. They got closer and they began to see the child's rags of clothes were covered in blood as well as her feet. All the while she let out blood curdling screams of "mommy, mommy!"

Rhapsody grasped her in her arms the child's and as she did the child's crying becoming more paced and controlled.

"Raven you need to look at this," Rhapsody said insistently.

"Yeah I know," he inquired "a little Necrolyte this far away from home is scary."

"Don't be foolish Raven - look closer this is not a necrolyte, look closely."

"Um whitish skin, long curly brown hair is there anything in particular I should be looking at?"

"There are no horns," insisted Rhapsody "Necrolytes, even young ones, have two horns on their head - at least some kind, yet as you see she doesn't."

"By the ancients you're right,"

"And her eyes they have a chocolate look to them; this is nothing like what a necrolytes eyes look like".

"Yeah isn't that an ention trait? But what would that mean?"

"I think were dealing with something big."

CHAPTER 9: DESOLATE CRY

Who are we to judge who is righteous and who is false? The liars from the saints. For you see the only true difference between your savior and a defiler is what side you see.

-Elrich

"These trions were worthless," laughed Cassanova "Hardly any fun at all killing them."

He looked around the room stepping over the sea green and blue bodies.

"Such a waste I mean come on, you could have been sporting you know. Now Elrich gets all the time he wants to torture your leader and there isn't anything you worthless sacks of meat can do about it."

Inside a small office of the minor defense tower was one of the great leaders of the Trion navy. His lime green skin was sweating in fear as his pink eyes stared back into cold black ones.

"You're considered one of the Night Blades best captains aren't you?"

The trion began to shake with fear.

"Something tells me you will crack under the slightest bit of pressure."

Yyou ddon't sscare me," the trion said.

But those cold black eyes stared back at him so unforgiving in nature.

"I will teach you the meaning of the word fear."

Elrich raised his hands and the Trion's screams filled the air.

"You can feel it can't you?" his voice remained monotone. "It's like a thousand knives cutting into your skin. It hits all the nerves without destroying them. In so doing I can do this for hours on end."

The poor trion's screams grew louder and louder, and blood gradually seemed to come out of his pores.

"Now you're going to tell me where the girl is."

"What girl," screamed the trion?

"The one you found in the tower - where is she?"

"I don't know…what you're talking about."

The hand lowered and the trion slumped over panting with such force as to think he would soon pass out.

"You really don't know do you?"

Elrich lifted his head

"You're a sick freak do you know that?" the trion spoke, "Your soul will be destroyed."

Elrich looked at him, and with what seemed like a strain forced a smile across his face.

"So you're not afraid to die?"

"I'd rather die than do anything to betray my people."

Elrich reached into the pocket of his robe. And he pulled out the black handle and looked at it for a moment.

"You know this weapon can take the shape of what weapon I may choose. You didn't give in. and as such your death will be quick."

The blade shot out black energy and struck the trion in the head."

Elrich unlocked the door and walked past the carnage with little care of anything else.

"Where to now?" Cassanova said.

"We must now head to the last known location that her healing has been used."

"You don't mean?"

"I do - a two man army is going to take down a major tower filled to the brim with kells. Fresh off of a battle against the trions."

"You know with that in mind they might just be able to fend us off."

"Now that sounds like a plan."

Cassanova smiled, a wide and menacing looking smile.

CHAPTER 10: LIEBEN

Rhapsody sat in a make shift chair stitching away at what seemed to be like a little home made rag doll. She had cut her fingers multiple times in the process of trying to sew up the little doll. But at long last the little creation was finally nearing completion and was quite lovely in a very odd sense of the word. It was constructed from leftover leather that raven had made for clothes, and was filled with sand.

She put the finishing touches on it then got up and walked outside of the house where the little girl was watching a squirrel pick up nuts and run back into the tree. Then scurry back down and pick up some more nuts. She watched with an almost eerie intensity. And then with a leap she jumped up into the air and caught the little squirrel by the tail. Quickly the little beast turned around and bit her on the hand and ran off as the little girl cried out in pain.

Rhapsody quickly ran up to examine the hand of the little girl but to her shock. The bite was gone. Nothing not even a mark left on her body to indicate that she had been bitten at all.

"Are you okay child. Does it hurt?"

The little girl shook her head no and held the little doll in her hands.

"You know its so prettiful mama. Thank you for making it for me I love it." they embraced, and Rhapsody felt a sort of warmth flood over her. It was like a love feeling but to one that she couldn't begin to sum up into any sort of words.

The little girl let go and began to run into the house. Rhapsody stared and smiled for a while. Taking time to enjoy the moment that she had just felt and what sort of significance it seemed to have on her.

"Hey Rhapsody, you mind if we go off somewhere to talk?" Raven asked as he came walking up with a boar in hand. "I hope you don't mind but I have something that I really would like to say to you. And I don't think it can wait."

"Yeah Raven anything you say."

They walked side by side deeper into the forest. Steps taking they naturally came closer together. With a shaking hand Raven grasped her hand. She smiled and looked at him with violet eyes full of joy. He smiled and they kept walking in silence.

"Raven where are we going anyway. Don't you think that we should be there too look after that little girl."

Raven smiled shyly.

"You know that was something I wanted to talk to you about."

"What about the child Raven? Do you not want her around because if that's the case well then I just can't allow that. I'll leave if that's what it takes..."

Raven gently touched her shoulders and smiled into her eyes.

"There is no way I would ever let that child leave. Nor would I allow harm to come to it. Though I don't want it to detract from what we have."

"What are you trying to say Raven?" Rhapsody said nervously.

Raven kissed Rhapsody slowly and passionately on the lips. He embraced her not forcefully, but enough so that she felt secure in her arms.

"What I'm trying to say Rhapsody is that I love you. And I always have. You've always been there for me. Now we have this child on our hand. I don't know how to react to it honestly on one part I love on how mothering your being towards to her. Yet on another hand I don't want to lose you. I want us both to be able to love each other. Hopefully with the same strength that you love that little girl."

Rhapsody smiled. She fully embraced Raven and held him for a long time.

"Raven sometimes you really are foolish aren't you? I've always loved you, the same as I love that little girl and I will always be there for both you and her so long as I live."

They held each other close kissing passionately, talking and letting their hands linger as they tend to do at times. And in the dim coolness of the setting sun two souls who had both been to afraid of their own feelings gave in and let their desires fall into beautiful consummation.

CHAPTER 11: A RARE GIFT

Does life exist - how would you know? Would you be able to count its worth? Or even when it no longer needs to go on?

"This child is indeed quite a rarity you know," Starseeker said "Plus she looks very cute as well."

"Thank you sweeker," the little girl said.

"You're quite welcome little girl, now finish your stew so that I can show you the zodiac."

"The Zodiac?"

"Yes my dear its how you can predict your life."

"pwedict my wife?"

"Yes deary, you see we kells have created a system to allow people to know what they're best at and what they should do with their life."

"So it kinda says what their life is?"

"For lack of a better word, yes I guess you could say that."

She finished the stew and placed it on a little well.

"And you say you don't remember anything that happened to you before hand?"

"No grandpa all up until mommy found me in a field about a month ago." She turned and began to walk toward the main room, where a large amount of astronomy equipment was. "Which one is the zodiac grandpa?" she asked looking through the various items. "Is this it grandpa?" the little girl asked holding up what seemed like a telescope.

"No not that!!!!" shouted Seeker as he ran over to go get the item from the little girl. He grabbed it and then gently set it on a side table. To which the item then fell over and cracked on the ground.

"No my dear," he said picking up the pieces of broken scope and setting them to where they would be safe. "This is called a telescope. It allows me to see the stars in all their glory and pureness" He then picked up a little cylindrical tube and popped it open.

"This poster here is a chart of our zodiac in its entirety, little one. It consists of three different things. There are sixteen animals each coordinating to their month of origin. Now the year is coordinated in an eight symbol with each one being represented by various clans that have existed over the years. And there are thirty-two days which are represented by various every day items."

"Really gwandpa,"

"Oh quite sure, see since you don't know when exactly you were born, we'll use the day that we found you so you were born in the month of the shark, and in the year of that of Urutso clan, and lastly." He said all of this never even looking the entire chart once. And the day should be that of a pair of wolf riding reins."

"Weines?"

"Yes my dear they allow you to be able to control wild beasts and ride them, to make a curse a gift so to speak."

"Hey grandpa you're not showing the little one anything she should be seeing should you?" Rhapsody said, walking and holding a large amount of wood between her arms. "This firewood should be enough for us to last a week." She said setting it down next to the fireplace.

"MOMMY!!" and the little girl went running toward open arms.

"Oh my sweet baby how have you been?"

"I've been great mommy see this morning I got up and I caught a little frog. He looks so cute mommy, but granpa said that I am apposed to let him go. And then he showed me some weally neato stuff."

"Hee hee, now remember Rhapsody the girl has to learn of culture at some point in her life, why not that of the people who will raise her?"

"Seeker, can I please speak to you in private?" asked Rhapsody gesturing her hand to the next room.

"Um okay," the old kell wobbled to the next room with Rhapsody right behind him. And with a close of a little wooden door the two began to speak in hushed whispers.

"You really think its wise to teach her about a group of people that exiled you and your son?"

"I think if the girl is to know of anything of a culture it should be our culture - that of my people who for unfortunate circumstances felt it was necessary to banish us."

"But why would you teach about a group like that?"

"Well its because there are things about this world that I have yet to tell my own son. So I think I should ask you if you can keep a secret."

"Wounds cut and yet they bleed no more. Its seems as if I must do much to sacrifice this holy light of love."

Raven said while tending some scratches that had somehow gotten across his right arm. He lay in a spring under a great willow where the coolness of the water and wind consumed him as his thoughts moved freely from one spot to the other.

"Why did we just let a little girl walk into our home? She seems nice and she likes playing with the old man. And Rhapsody looks to her as her own little girl. But I just can't fight the feeling that I can't get my head around that it's not a good thing. And I mean the little girl comes up and looks at me like I'm strange. Like I'm some kind of monster and I don't even know what I did to make her think of me like that."

Raven rose up from the pool and gave a great howl that echoed throughout the scope of the forest. He turned his head and he noticed the little curly haired girl who was wearing a baggy brown dress made from the leather of some great beast.

"Um Mr. Waven can I talk to you?" the little girl asked while walking up to the well.

"I don't see why not kid. You know this place is so close to our home, I'm surprised we don't bathe everyday kid." He got up but limped a bit as he tried to get out. He lay down. "Just got a little hurt in a hunt. Nothing much to worry about."

"But mister your still bleeding." The little girl said pointing to his leg.

"Its fine kid it fine."

The little girl walked up to him. She came into the little pond and gave Raven a big hug. Then there was a flash of white light and then Raven's wounds were healed with no sign of ever being damaged at all.

"By the Zodiac kid, what did you do?" Raven exclaimed looking at his wounds. "How were you able to do that?"

The girl looked at her arms shocked. She moved them this way and that with hands glowing of white light.

"I don't know!!!"

CHAPTER 12: AN INVASION OF TWO

And so a demon did pour through the plain; did wreak hell throughout the whole of the world.

The fourth tower was a great building that was over forty stories tall. Held straight with giant chains that went down to the base. As well as a great base that seemed to appear like the roots of some great tree.

It began to rain during the midday and all about the land there lay an eerie sort of feel to it. Then great amphibians riding upon giants that seemed to be a mix between crocodiles, but with legs under their bodies instead of out to their sides. They seemed to be much bigger as well, about the size of small horses. Giant flying Rays moved slowly and gracefully from the sky. Six in all, they were great creatures, three of whom held soldiers in a giant basket while the other three appeared to have cannons and the men who operated them. And out of the tower fireballs whizzed through the air heading towards this impending army of Trions.

Meanwhile in the shadows two characters stood cloaked under the cover of great ramps that let people come in and out of the tower.

"This is quite interesting," Cassanova said. "So this means somewhere in there is someone who can find this child?"

Elrich turned to face his birdlike companion.

"I am quite certain the information we seek will be among the people of this citadel. We just need to know how to extract it from the creatures.

Cassanova's face gave a dark grin.

"My methods or yours?"

Elrich looked towards the sky. The firing of fireballs out of the tower, and the cannon balls that drew ever closer to the tower.

"Lets see here." Said Elrich "The kells have two vantage points to exit this building while the trions have to play by those same gates so the bulk of men will come from either side. Now if we simply make even more of an emphasis I could use that to sneak around and get to the information records from there I simply get someone to kindly point me in the right direction."

"Kindly? Now that seems more like my style doesn't it?" said Cassanova grinning "personally I think I know who should be the runner to get both sides to look one way."

"Yes," said Elrich "I was thinking of the same thing. I think this will be your time to shine Cassanova have fun."

Cassanova began to laugh a hardy powerful laugh.

The gates opened from either side of the tower and an eruption of yelling came and a large number of kells came running from the tower. Elrich held Cassanova back

"You must wait till a decent number of them are out so you don't end up allowing the trions to take too much of an offensive. Remember the longer this battle lasts, the more time it will allow us to complete our goals.

"Now can I go?" asked Cassanova.

Elrich waved his hand "Do what you will; just try not to get yourself killed, will you?"

Cassanova jumped into the air and landed on top of the wing that the kells poured out of in such great numbers.

"Now for the fun."

And Cassanova drew two swords and plunged head long into an oncoming group of kells. Decapitating foe after foe that stood before him. They got around and surrounded him. Surrounded by spear and sword, he dropped his weapons and began to chant to himself.

"What the hell?" asked one of the kells from in front. "Is he trying to pray?" as the chanting continued the weapons rose little bit from the ground until they were waist length to each kell soldier.

"And now," spoke Cassanova very coldly "You die, fools who didn't strike."

The swords began to spin furiously around cutting kell after kell that was close enough to get struck. And as they fell so they became a part of this cursed twister that was flowing. And it grew large and extremely powerful in its wake.

Meanwhile a hooded figure with ram horns turned to look over his shoulder.

"So he seems to be doing a fine job distracting the foot soldiers. Now we'll see about this battle."

At that very moment a trion general wearing a cape raised a trident into the air, and all the men behind him shouted and charged foreword.

The wolf riders from the scouting now charged dead ahead towards the trions at such a speed that they seemed like a blur. Screeches came from above Elrich and out of pure curiosity he looked up to see giant wolflike bats flying through the air. They were flying out of the tower and it seemed as if they were heading for the giant rays and the ever advancing trion army. The Rays tried to duck and move but to no avail; they were too slow and soon a number of bats grasped tight onto the ray and began to bite and gnaw away at the creature. Trions fought the bats off shaking a few as they did. But the growing number was too much and the ray fell from the air and crashed to the ground. Though before it did, all of the bats scampered off the mighty beast. A great cheer echoed throughout the tower now as a great number of civilians began to shout with joy as they saw the great ray fall and then finally crash head first into the ground.

"Fools, they don't have any idea of what's coming, but it doesn't much matter what does matter is that I really need to get one of those bats as my own." mumbled Elrich. The kells appeared to be holding their own on the ground when more foot soldiers began to power from the tower and began to drive headlong into the fray.

But as they came, so did two powerful rays that shot straight down like lightning and slammed into the various wings, scooping kells into their mouths.

"How interesting - wonder what the rays do with the parts that they can't digest."

The rays flew back to the kells who were finding ways around were bombarded with the weapons, armor, and bones of their former comrades.

"Fast digestion I can see why the trions are so fond of using them in battle."

The bats however were quick to respond. Even though they outnumbered the rays, the horse-sized bats could not stand up to the massive flying rays, which seemed much too large to be killed them before they were able to do some damage. One of the giant rays now smashed against the side of the tower as he was being taken down by the bats.

Then a ray flew down near Elrich and as smooth as air Elrich grabbed hold of the tail and climbed onto it as one of the bats came down. Upon further looking, Elrich noticed a wolf-like face on the beast. He kicked the rider off of the creature, and then he grabbed hold of the creature and used his dark magic until the creature did as he wanted.

Meanwhile Cassanova jumped out of the fully created cyclone that he had created and ran headlong into the battle with the trions and kells, shouting and whooping with swords in hand.

"This is one of the best days ever!!!" Cassanova shouted as he pulled an axe from the ground and swung the huge weapon with delight.

All the while Elrich led the bat through a random window and into the stone tower. Torches kept the building lit up and carpets covered various areas. Yet the stone seemed to have a large effect on the overall castle like appearance of the tower.

"Now I wonder - where is the record room?"

"Hmm a very good question indeed." A Kell said emerging from the next room over.

He wore a long black robe lined with pictures of fire and water. "I see you came here from less than loyal allies. What is your reason for being here?"

Elrich reached into his pocket.

"I've come here in search of information about a girl."

The kells eyes widened and a smile came across his face.

"Well I happen to know about a little girl, what would you say that we have a little bet?"

Elrich stared for a moment calculating the next move.

"And if I should lose?"

"Then you must tell me where the forest in which the twin thrones are."

"And why would a Kell want to know where the matriarch and Czar are?"

"Oh I have my reasons young Necrolyte, you will find that you will give me this information regardless of the outcome of this fight."

Elrich raised his katana handle and nodded his head.

"I shall accept your challenge."

"Good, its been so long since I sensed an opponent quite as powerful as you."

"Who are you anyway, Kell?!"

"I am Falhuman, son of a god but bound to the kells until the time is right for me to serve the whole of Vestric."

"So gods love dogs, hmm - seems interesting."

Falhuman reached into his robe pocket and removed a white handle that appeared to be that of a katana, with two dice hanging from the hilt.

"White bone of an angel, Pure in nature, it draws from purity and it allows energy to convert pure and bend to whatever form I chose."

"Interesting - so you can draw and convert souls to a specific energy level around you."

"While yours just takes and converts with pain and beats them into submission."

A white beam came from the handle and Falhuman came rushing at Elrich. Elrich activated his sword and the black energy clashed with the white in a stunning display. Falhuman sidestepped and slashed the blade at Elrichs back. But a black sort of shield covered the energy from being able to hit.

Flahumans smile grew larger.

"You truly are a creature of darkness aren't you?"

And the black energy slammed down against the white. Falhuman grabbed hold of the dice dangling and snapped them off and chucked them.

"Now you get to see a brand new trick.

The energy from Falhuman's hilt went from white to blue and slammed Elrich into the back of a wall.

"You see every time I throw the dice energy will convert itself into something else and than return it to me for another shot." He said while holding his weapon to the side so he could show that the dice were now dangling from his blade once again.

Elrich pushed himself away from the wall and ran straight towards to the window as Falhuman began to shoot orbs of pressured water.

"You know you're quite good, but I have a little trick up my sleeve as well. RENTIOR!!!"

Elrich's legs became surrounded with black energy and his speed grew tenfold. In a flash he was behind Falhuman whom he punched with an arm in dark energy. And the kell was sent against the wall at the same moment that a giant ray flew against the tower with a crash. The creature began to drag across the concrete breaking a giant hole in the wall where the two enemies were fighting.

People began to cheer again as they saw that this second creature was being brought down. The tail caught Falhuman by his robe and he was swept up. Regaining his balance, he situated himself on the falling ray, gesturing with his hand for Elrich to come chasing after him.

Elrich charged all his energy into his legs and began to sprint towards the side of the building and then leapt through the air landing safely on the Rays back. Falhuman swung at Elrich as soon as he landed on the ray. The two forms of energy crashed in an instant. The ray began to gain a little motion back and it began to soar away from the tower and around to the center of the field where the hull of the battle was taking place. Elrich focused his energy back to his feet and swung down the blade in a distraction move and tripped Falhuman. He fell backwards, throwing his sword out in an offensive that threw Elrich off of his back. He used this time so that he could get back to his feet and steady himself on the rocking beast.

"That was a cheap move Necrolyte."

Elrich looked at his opponent callously, And a greater amount of the dark energy seemed to surround the hilt now.

"Thought you wanted a good fight Falhuman?"

A smile went across the kell's face.

"Yeah, and so far you seem pretty good, so far that is." Falhuman said as he threw the dice towards Elrich.

Falhuman charged forward, his handle flashing a brilliant red aura. Elrich met him this time and the combined attack split the ray in two, a front half and a back half.

"Rio Ranpawn," Shouted Elrich and an entity completely black in color shot toward the other half of the ray where Falhuman was situated. He landed on it as it was plummeting exponentially but he could not see where Falhuman was.

Than a great fireball hit Elrich in the head. The energy dissipated from the dark energy that was swirling around Elrich. Then the Energy focused to his back until great wings sprung from his back and he flew in the air flying toward where the fireball had originated. As he flew higher Elrich came to the scary conclusion that Falhuman had made it to the top of the tower.

"You know Necrolyte you're quite the warrior. What is you name?"

Elrich reached the top and began to look around the flat topped surface for something that looked like his opponent. He looked out towards the battle. The rain fell with lightning flashes dotting the sky. Fireballs and cannons were going this way and that and overall it appeared that the kells might just be able to drive off the great number of invaders that were now upon their doorsteps.

Falhuman appeared in a flash behind him, his smile broad.

"Please tell me your name young warrior I need to remember you."

Elrich turned, unfazed by the kell's quickness.

"I am Elrich, a Necrolyte trained in the art of mastering necromancy."

"But have you, Elrich? Mastered necromancy I mean."

"I still have much to learn, this is true - but I feel I am better versed then some of my peers. And I have more than enough skill to defeat someone like you."

"You know you say it, but you say it with very little emotion, young Elrich. It's almost as if you have no care at all.

"I apologize if you are put off but I assure you that I am taking this fight seriously."

"Then why is it, if your magic is to use the body to the limits causing it increased power, speed, and strength and cunning … so why have you not tried to use your abilities on me to cause excruciating pain?"

"You seem like a good opponent, so I would not try to use such cheap tactics."

"Interesting – well, I bet you can guess what the dice landed on when I threw them while you were sight seeing."

The white handle spurted a dark energy that erupted from the handle.

"Let's test your skills then."

Falhuman leapt back and then ran towards Elrich with a note of seriousness on his face. He slashed down with full force upon Elrichs blade and the two began a dance of blade as each one struggled and pushed their bodies to the brink and back. Flashes of black and destruction were all around now as bits and pieces of the roof were being ripped apart by the intense duel. Then the two clashed and held strength fast as each one tried to exert more energy into the blade so that they would envelop the other.

"Alright," said Falhuman "I'll tell you the last place we had the little girl before we lost track of her."

The two stood down and the energy receded from the two handles.

"What's so special about this little girl anyway?" Elrich enquired.

"Well, when we found her she could revive an elder without any of the shady after effects that have come with necromancy. As well as the ability to heal scars and other wounds without any problems."

"So she's like an anti Necromancy user?"

"Yes, completely - and when she felt threatened she managed to bring down a chorus of winged creatures that killed everyone around them without any pain."

"So this is holy magic? And to such a degree I never thought possible in someone so young. Or anyone for that matter."

"There's more - she was able to grasp other forms of magic; for a young child the magic that she can wield is beyond belief."

Elrich bowed to Falhuman

"Thank you but if I may why did you just give up the fight."

"I didn't," Falhuman shrugged "We fought to equal degrees, I have merely postponed this fight until a later date, young Elrich."

Elrich turned and began to walk away. Falhuman stamped his foot.

"We had a deal; where are the two thrones?"

Elrich turned to look at him before he left.

"They are in the grave of my family and friends. They were buried there because of me. I must do what I do so that I can bring honor to their souls. By any means necessary."

Falhuman stood smiling.

"Why would you do such a thing?"

"Because if I don't do that I also stand the chance that so many others could be killed by this ruthless god. So I need to attain a godlike state through any means. And this god resides in the Shadow forest close to where the western sea lies."

"Hmm, she was last seen near Dalcohn forest."

Elrich then snuck away with Cassanova into the darkness that now eclipsed this war torn land.

CHAPTER 13: THE LIGHT OF A NAME

Names are something I think most other races take for granted. You know they are all born at birth with their name already picked out and they don't even get to choose. The Kells however do name themselves at a date when we truly know what connotation we want to have. We are in many ways allowed to be who we want to be because we are able to label and choose who we are and what we shall be called.

The little girl stared awestruck, looking through the glinting telescope.

"Where does the stars go in the morning grampa?"

The old kell hobbled over.

"Well my dear when our closest star rises, then its own grand light blights out that of all other stars in the area."

The little girl looked awed in wonder.

"So there's another star that's so bright you can't see any others."

"Well I guess you could say that. Maybe the other stars try to bring light to our area but only one truly can. Maybe this star is special above the others because its our lightbringer?" the kell said smiling as he patted the girls head.

"So only one can be a lightbringer? Grampa I'm kinda hungwy can I have some stoup?"

"Sure you can little one I'll make some right now.

Rhapsody walked into the room, yawning as she did. There seemed something quite peculiar about her. Raven walked in from hunting with a large deer over his shoulders. He looked stunned at Rhapsody.

"Rhapsody what happened your scars are gone?"

Rhapsody looked at her arms and with a shock everyone began to look at her. Rhapsody was speechless her whole body frozen.

"T-this is a miracle," she breathed "How did it happen."

The little girl skipped over to her and with a smile on her face she went up and hugged Rhapsody around her hips.

"I make scwatches go away mommy."

Rhapsody knelt down teary eyed.

"But how little one were you able to do it?"

"I made an angel show up mommy and he said he would heal my mommy," the little girl said.

"But little one," Rhapsody asked "What exactly is an angel?"

"An angel mommy," the little girl said very matter of factly. "Is a pale skinned person like me and you, and even daddy. They have as beautiful eyes as mommy and they have these huge white wings and they fly down and help me when I need it most. They talk to me. Tell me what to do."

They became shocked, each person looking back and forth at another trying to figure out what she meant by this.

Star seeker hobbled over to Rhapsody and patted Rhapsody on the back.

"Raven, I know you may not like it but I think you should consider letting her go through the ceremony."

Raven looked down at his feet.

"I guess she's one of us now. And with powers like this people with less than honorable goals might be looking for her. These past few months have been something special haven't they? We'd best get things prepared, then." Raven then ran out of the house quickly.

Rhapsody looked down at star seeker.

"So what kind of things do we usually have to get for a naming ceremony?"

"Well my dear, it all depends on how much money the particular family possesses. It's usually a festive event. But in our case I think such things would be a luxury, so we'll just make the basics - which is a scroll of parchment and something like a knife."

Why a knife?" asked Rhapsody

"Well," said the old kell "The name is written with ones own blood."

"How barbaric," protested Rhapsody.

"Its okay mommy," the little girl spoke up. "The angels will make it better."

And then she began to skip toward the same room that Raven had came through.

He stood in the small room with what looked like an elongated machete.

"Kid," Raven said earnestly "I want you to grab that dagger that is lying on the floor."

The little girl did so.

"Now let's head back to Rhapsody and Seeker."

"But," she said.

"No buts, kid," his words were a bit broken they pertained an edge of fear in them. "Just do as you're told; I'll explain everything after the ceremony."

They both walked back out and with absolute silence Raven laid the sheet of parchment on the table that had been cut from the great tree that was their home."

"I don't mean to seem rude but we really have to do this fast, please."

"Whats wrong?" Rhapsody asked.

The four gathered around the table quickly, each taking a corner.

"Now we recite the ancient prayer," said Star Seeker. "We exist in time and space." The others repeated these words. "Now we find one that has grown." Raven and Seeker did a motion to indicate that they should hold hands. "We are united in our resolve as one." A pause. "And now we find one who has the ability to become one with the pack now and forever." The group said amen and the little one was raised up onto the table.

The girl put her finger in her mouth and though hard.

"Well," she said profoundly, "my second name will be Lightbringer. Cause it's the star that allows us to have sunny and happy days." The group smiled. Raven even gave a mild chuckle.

"That's a good choice, my daughter." Raven said, blushing. All three smiled.

"Honey it's taken you so long to say something like that."

"I know, I guess I'm a stubborn fool."

The little girl ran over and gave Raven a big hug.

"Your so silly daddy," she said.

The old man held out the parchment and the dagger.

"Now we're going to have to prick your finger just a little bit."

They did and with Rhapsody guiding her hand they spelled out Lightbringer.

"Now little one for the tough part, you have to pick the name to which you will be called from now on. The little girl thought for a moment.

"I want to be called Rain."

The three looked at each other and each one beamed.

"Rain Lightbringer," said Raven.

"That's a very pretty name," said Rhapsody. There was a group hug and there was for that moment pure undaunted happiness. A family full of species and an unknown child. Now named and finally united.

CHAPTER 14: THE REQUIEM

We feel that there is one who knows much. But does she or her vision of the supposed truth make him blind by his own feelings?

That night started as a great celebration but with a crashing event it became very urgent. Raven had informed Rhapsody and Seeker he had caught the scent of something foul. And due to the fact one would have to protect Rain and Seeker, Rhapsody chose to lead them to an abandoned tower off to the west. They both dressed themselves in armor that they had from before the exile. Raven grabbed his best sword and made ready for battle.

"I love you Raven," Rhapsody had said.

"Good luck my son," Star Seeker told him.

"Goodbye daddy," Rain said holding on tight to him. "Your armor is cold, you're not as fluffy now daddy."

"I know kid," Raven said "Daddy's gonna miss you, but he'll see you again."

They rode away on that black wolf into the night.

Raven turned toward the forest. It was cold now, his breath visible on the chilly evening. He took a step foreword. He could see the sky clear and black. No stars out tonight. But a huge full moon gave an almost ominous appearance to the scene.

He had the scent now, it was dank and very strong, yet it was familiar. He moved with quiet swiftness. Through tall grass and bramble, over stumps and various debris.

There standing a few yards ahead of him was quite an intimidating looking kell. With a mask that covered the entire face. But there was something odd. The scent was distorted from what it should be.

"Brother," said the creature before him. "That bitch scarred me and then nearly killed me." Masked said pointing at him. "The least you could do is let me have some revenge. Or that cursed child you hold in your possession."

Raven stood up weapon drawn "You go to hell, Scream," Raven shouted back at her. He shouted a deafening roar to which fire burst from his mouth and the sound seemed to echo throughout the cold night.

"Hmm, interesting - has my little brother been training since those days when everyone used to beat you up?"

The two charged at each other, Raven's Sword and Scream's claws. Scream was moving faster than she ever had previously. Her feet moved like they were great emblems of power. She jumped into the air and then slashed Raven right across the left side of his face.

"That's for what that little bitch did to my face," Scream shouted.

She tripped Raven and he fell to the ground but he couldn't help but notice a great dark presence about her as he did.

"I need more power," Raven shouted. He threw his hands up to defend himself and shouted "Nekodah!" As Raven shouted, a huge fireball shot from his hand and knocked Scream backward. Raven jumped to his feet and held his hand over his sword.

"Kirin Tah," he said and the sword became covered in fire.

Then he ran towards Scream with everything he could muster. She lunged up and her hands became larger and engulfed in this dark energy.

The two were engaged in back and forth bashing neither one gaining ground over the other

"How did it feel Raven to know you never belonged in out society? That you were useless trash."

Raven felt the hate inside him grow with ever taunt. and his fire grow weaker. "You're a bastard child – you're a nothing. Useless and despised, you have nothing in our world or any world." Scream threw a punch and Raven went flying. She walked over and stared down at him as he tried to pull himself up from the hit.

"And the worst part of all, the part that even sickens me - you won't be able to save the people who actually might have given a shit about you. They're all going to die Raven, and it's your fault that you're too weak to save them."

Raven jumped into the air grabbing Scream as he did. The area around him was burning now in flame. His roars of anger grew louder as they climbed over the trees and with a yell he kicked Scream away from him and through a surging fireball that sent her body hurling towards the ground. Raven then floated down and picked up his Sword.

A necrolyte stood in front of him, hands in his robe. His black eyes seemed devoid of spirit.

"The art of dark magic. Pushing the body to its farthest extremes. You know if a soul is resiliant and sticks to where its body is, and can fight through the pain, they can walk again, talk again, live again." The Necrolyte turned his head. "I followed the trail of an Ention Caravan that was then attacked. There was thought to be no one alive. But I followed it further and then I found you.

"Here I am but if you want to find that one survivor she's not here."

"Yes I know she's exactly where I want her to be."

CHAPTER 15: AVIAN

to what lengths will one go to defend those that they love? Would they cheat? Lie? or even kill to know that the ones they love will be safe and sound?

The great two moons shined over the tower, casting eery shadows in the darkness of that cold stone building.

The wolf trotted, panting as he went. The three were scared, noises echoed through the old building, and the eery air was putrid and dead. The wind howled an eery song as it blew through the echoes of the once proud building.

"I'm scared mommy," Rain held tight onto Rhapsody. "I want to go home,"

"Hush now little one, we can't right now," Rhapsody said.

Laughing erupted throughout the building, it was horrible insidious dark laughter.

"Seeker, give me your sword," said Rhapsody, dismounting from the large wolf.

"You both may live if you if you hand over the girl," Shouted a voice that echoed throughout the building.

Suddenly a large Avian jumped down onto the first floor with a thud. It pulled a large sword from a pack of various large weapons it had with it.

Seeker tossed Rhapsody the sword which she held tightly in her hands.

"So the little girl thinks she's gonna bring me down?" Said the Avian called Cassanova.

"You touch a hair on my daughter's head and I'm gonna tear you apart."

Cassanova smiled.

"Alright lets see what you got little girl," Cassanova raised his sword and clanged it against hers, not budging. For nothing would shake Rhapsody's focus from her daughters life.

"So you do know how to fight then, don't you?"

He lept into the air, and digging his talons he began to crawl on the wall.

"You seem to enjoy cheating during a fight don't you?"

Cassanova jumped down talons bared, giving a huge screech, towards Seeker and the wolf.

Rhapsody crouched, then did a back flip and launched a kick that sent Cassanova flying backward.

"You won't lay a hand on her, you monster,"

Cassanova wiped blood away from his jaw and revealed a menacing smile.

"Oh we have barely begun to duel,"

Cassanova charged as fast as he could toward Rain.

The smash of his sword knocked Rhapsody's sword out of her hands as she went to defend. It landed with a clang that echoed throughout the now silent tower.

"Now I'm gonna end you."

Cassanova grabbed the sword by the foot and spinning around flung the sword into a constant spin around himself.

Rhapsody ducked the first revolution with little effort.

"Ourukia!" she shouted and the sword fell to the ground. Cassanova shouted with pain.

"Rigarka Claw," said Rhapsody and her right hand turned to that of a demonic bony hand, that was as sharp as steel.

She slashed her hand but Cassanova spun around. As he did various weapons went flying from his packs.

Rhapsody was pinned against the wall, her heart beating faster. She knew that this could very well spell the end for her. A sword was stabbed into her right arm; nowhere to go, nowhere to hide. Death was coming at last, this death that would leave all she cared about scarred like she once was, like she should have remained. She felt unwanted for most of her life. It was only in this last few months that she seemed to know and feel accepted and now this world was crashing down on her.

She could feel the warm blood oozing from her mouth with every breath she took. Her nose was bleeding badly, too. Her eyes were dazed with the lack of sight. Cassanova moved slowly, now strutting as he did over his new found victory.

"I told you, that you had no chance you little bitch. And you can't use any of your spells either. This is where you die."

Cassanova stared at her malformed body pinned up against the cold stone. His eyes were greedy with power.

"You know the mission can wait. First I'm gonna make you pay, you little shit."

Rhapsody became angry, her eyes full of instilled rage. She would have to find a way to end this fray here and now. She would have to find some way that she could emerge from this with victory for her and Rain.

Cassanova unsheathed his sword from his hilt and held it to her neck.

"Do you expect me to beg for death you slimy monster." Rhapsody said. She tilted her head back and spat blood into his face. "Go to hell you lousy piece of shit."

Cassanova became infuriated; he rammed his head against hers, bashing it into the concrete.

"You know I've waited for this moment when I could kill someone who cares oh so deeply in nothing."

"KIRIN TOR," Rhapsody said with a faint smile. Cassanova's body jerked. Then he fell over and landed on the cold stone with a thud.

"To complete the death spell one must be able to touch a single part of the body."

She then took her free hand and pulled the sword from her thigh and slowly unpinned herself. She took a few steps away from the Avian corpse and then collapsed upon the floor. Blood covered this place now. it seemed to flow like water after a long storm.

"Rain, run!!!!" she shouted, but she was too dazed to notice that Seeker had run as soon as the fighting had gotten intense. "I shouldn't tell Raven about this. He'd end up blaming himself for all of this. He cares so much, its hard to believe he took in someone like me for no other reason than his sheer kindness. But he remains ridden with this haunting banishment. My love, all you wanted was to belong. And now I have to leave you all alone, I hope you realize I don't want to." Tears were flowing from her eyes. She tried so desperately to try and get up but she couldn't. She collapsed again on the floor. "I'm so sorry everyone that I have to go but I want you too know I really wish that I could stay for just a little longer." Her heart beat slower and slower until it stopped completely and she left the company of the mere mortals and entered the endless abyss.

CHAPTER 16: THE POWER OF THE SOUL

What is a soul? Do we know how to rate the matters of how pure a spirit is? That they may become able to judge who is righteous and who is not.

Raven stared into those cold black eyes.

"If everything is as it should be than you have already lost." said Elrich.

Raven closed his eyes, tears falling as he did. The tear dropped to the earthy ground only to be evaporated in an instant as Raven's body became surrounded by blue flames.

"No," Raven said through his teeth. "No its not true," his body was shaking now with fury. "I can save them, dammit." Raven jumped into the air and he shot through the air looking like a comet.

His speed was unmatchable as he cut the night air like a streak of star. From the distance growing ever closer he saw the tower on the horizon

He went through the top window and landed on some old moldy carpet with a thud.

"I can't smell Rain or dad but," He ran down the stairs as fast as he could, and when he reached the bottom he ran right next to Rhapsody's body.

Raven stood for a moment caught in this horrifying grip of disbelief that gripped him like a sword through the chest.

"I was too late. If only I could have gotten there sooner, if only I could have found a way to save the ones that are closest to me. I won't let the same fate overcome Rain or my father."

"Oh what a shame," said that same cold voice from the forest. "She was a very beautiful creature, you know that. I'm sure you loved her very much didn't you?"

Raven rose slowly, fire now surrounding a large area around him. He turned and pointed the sword directly at Elrich.

"Don't you have a soul, you monster?" Raven asked.

Elrich stared for a moment then reached into the right pocket of his robe and removed a crystal vial, which looked very fancy in shape. The liquid inside was light blue with an aura coming from the vial.

"Its right here." Elrich said rather plainly. "You see if I use only the souls around me, not only can I gather more energy ... but that energy doesn't take from my soul or hurt it in anyway."

"You're one sick freak, you know that?"

Elrich shrugged. From his left pocket he drew the tooth of the demon.

"I'm smart, and I'll be the one who sends you to the grave."

Elrich slashed the tooth and a wave of black energy came from the handle and spurting towards Raven.

"Now die Kell!!!!!"

But the attack merely dissipated as it hit against a large wall of flame that rose up around Raven.

"No, you will be the one to die. NODAKAH!!!!" A large fireball shot from the tip of the sword; Elrich jumped out of the way but found Raven had predicted this move and the two clashed weapons and eyes met. One cold and soulless, The other filled with rage and anger.

Elrich's legs than became black and he ran to one end of the tower and he jumped off the wall and propelled himself toward Raven. Raven created a frieball that surrounded himself, providing a shield.

Elrich smashed bit by bit at the shield with the demon tooth. Then

Raven burst fire around and sent Elrich back against the wall. Raven leapt and was at Elrich at the other end of the tower. He slashed the sword and with a roar of rage, he slashed hard against Elrich's chest.

Elrich then kicked Raven in the chest, then he uppercutted Raven. Elrich sprung a tail using his dark magic and using this tail he slammed Raven into a wall. Elrich walked slowly over to Rhapsody's body.

He rubbed his hand on Rhapsody's face. "You know yourself to be one lucky guy. I mean she's a real good-looking woman, and those beautiful purple eyes. What a shame.

Raven slashed Elrich now across his back. Elrich's robe fell to the ground and blood seemed to completely cover Elrich's torso. Elrich shouted.

"You lousy animal, I'll tear you limb from limb!"

Elrich rose; weapons smashed against one another. Eyes of pure hate interlocked with the soulless menace, as the two drew more power and used it to push the other over the edge.

Smaash!!!! Raven lifted up his foot. The little glass vial that had contained the soul was smashed on the ground and nothing was left of its contents but the glass that held it.

The two looked at each other.

Raven with various cuts and bruises all across his body. His armor dented and bent, his face bloody and his fur mangled.

Elrich stared back. His body with various burns, his robes chopped and gone. All that remained was his waist sash holding the article of clothing on, and a huge cut lining down his grey chest and back.

"Why is it you care so much about this girl - what does she mean to you?"

"She means the world. Ever since she came into my life it's been better. No it hasn't just been better. It's been something great something more pure. And I'll give my life if I have to. To defend the people that I care about."

"And so you now give your life in hopes that it will help them?"

Elrich's face stayed firm his face stiff.

"I'll make a difference, Necrolyte - I will bury you beneath my blade here and now."

Raven swung his blade towards Elrichs head. His right horn was cut straight off of his head and landed with a thud.

"AAAAAHHH," shouted Elrich, clutching on the right side of his head.

"I'll kill you!" Elrich swung madly but could not hit the target in front of him. Raven stood back and red energy started massing around his hands.

"Destruction," Raven shouted. Then massive fireball flew from his hands, Elrich still clutching the side of his head, put as much energy as he could to cut the oncoming fireball in two. He then seemed to almost vanish for a blip and then appear in front of Raven. His blade-slashed blood flew, and Raven fell to his knees.

"I will always remember you, kell," Elrich said. "We are so... different. You proved to be my toughest opponent yet."

Raven's eyes were awe struck. Elrich stood before the dying warrior and bowed his head.

"It's a real shame they exiled one of the most powerful kells I've ever met."

Then Elrich walked away into the darkness.

Raven with what little strength he had clawed his way to where Rhapsody's body lay.

The night sky looked peaceful now to Raven. He could see the many stars the few moons. One of them was even full, its great light shining upon the tower revealing it in a soothing white light.

"It's a bright moon, my love. That means I can find you... You are my swan, the swan that was so graceful and beautiful and gave time to the once sad and lonely Raven."

And just like that Raven drew his last breath. And he and Rhapsody were stars in the sky of the night, their love for each other only eclipsed by that of the LightBringer.

CHAPTER 17: A NEW LIGHT

And then brother sun did steal his place from the brother darkness but this would only be for a borrowed time of bliss.

The wolf raced on, its speed unmatched. He never stopped, nor tired. Through grass and forest, over hills and valleys journeying the wolf running towards his never ending goal of safety from and evil that never stopped.

Star Seeker held on to Rain and the wolf with all his might.

"Grandpa where are we, where are we going?"

"Somewhere far away my dear, somewhere you'll be safe and sound.

There was a crash of lightning and in that brief time of light the wolf came to a screeching halt. There, standing in front of them was a hooded kell. His bright yellow eyes, peered out from the hood.

"Falhuman?" asked Star Seeker

"Yes it is I, the one who trained your son. How are you faring this evening?"

"What kind of question is that?"

"Well I thought it was a simple one. The point being is that I'm going to tell you where to put the girl so that she'll be safe."

"Oh and why should I trust you?"

"Well, your son would do it if I asked him to. And if I'm not mistaken he was like a father to this little girl. I think he would trust my ideas, don't you think?"

Star Seeker looked at Rain for a little while.

"What do you think we should do, Rain?"

The little girl looked up, eyes full of innocence.

"We should listen to him Grampa, I think he knows."

"Okay, then I'll trust your decision." Said Star Seeker "Tell me what you want me to do now, Falhuman.

"Okay," said Falhuman. "Follow me."

Falhuman shot off into the night with such speed that the wolf was barely able to keep behind it.

"There is an Ention convoy over this way she will be safe among them."

Star Seeker was puzzled by this but he never slowed down the wolf for a second. They went over a hill and could see in front of them a group of entions who had set up camp.

"It is here that the one who shall raise her from now on will live."

"Will she be safe among them?"

"I'm sure," responded Falhuman and they slowed down their pace as they walked into the camp.

"I have returned Noustrous with the child, just as I promised.

From a large tent came an average size dark skinned man with long hair. He walked toward the group; he had a gentle look about him in a way that seemed to make others around you calmer.

"Ah at last, I thank you kind soul, though I do feel awful for asking such a high price." Said Noustrous.

"Its okay Noustrous," Falhuman said placing his hands on his shoulders

"It's not your fault your wife is barren and besides you so often helped me that I should, no I owe you this."

Rain stepped down slowly from the wolf.

"Hello child what is your name?" asked Noustrous very kindly.

The girl walked slowly up to Noustrous.

"My name is Rain. Are you going to take care of me until mommy and daddy come and get me?"

The man smiled and took her in his arms.

"My dear I will protect you everyday until they come back to get you." Noustrous turned to Falhuman and smiled. "Thank you so much. I'll never forget your kindness Falhuman"

"Think nothing of it; I will keep in touch with you though,"

The man smiled. "I wouldn't expect anything else from you."

"Oh!" said Star Seeker he dug into the saddlebag and pulled from it a book and a rag doll.

"The book is a collection of poems her father made. And her mother sewed this rag doll specifically for her. So please let her have them. It would mean the world to me."

He handed them to the man who happily obliged. Then Falhuman and Seeker left in silence. The night was quiet and as one rode and the other walked. There seemed to be a great calm about everything. Falhuman was the first to break the silence.

"You're going to come back to the tower and live the rest of your days with your old job back. Rest assured her attackers will not come after her again I have dealt with that."

"What about Rhapsody and my son?"

"They are true heroes. They're probably some of the greatest people I've ever met. They were able to give their lives for something much bigger than either of them could know. And they lived better lives than many others hope to. I'm truly sorry, but I think giving you your home back and your old job back is the least I can do."

Star Seeker turned to Falhuman, tears beginning to fall from his face. He rode into the remnants of the darkness. The old day dying, but a new one rising little by little to bring a new time ... a new age. And even though it may seem to be covered in darkness there will always be a light bringer.

EPILOGUE: ELRICH'S TALE

One must be able to rise from the ashes like the phoenix who no sooner than it bursts into flames is able to fly back into this world in screaming majesty.

White walls, White bed, white, white, and more white. Body bandaged, bruised scars that will probably never go away. What a sense of defeat that seems to come over one self

Elrich lay in bed, reading a book entitled the Two Half Moons.

"Nurse, oh nurse!" Elrich said.

A small avian wearing a summer dress came walking into the white atrocity that Elrich was forced to call his room.

"What is it Mr. Elrich?"

"Well it would appear that I am fully healed - can I go now?"

"Well it would appear most of your minor burns are gone, but the two cuts on your front and back won't go away. As well as the fact that you'll have to live your life with one horn."

"That's okay, I would rather keep them. I need to remember that day." Elrich put a piece of paper in the book and turned to nurse. "Please allow me some time to stretch my legs a bit then? I hope that isn't too much to ask for?"

The nurse looked at him then smiled.

"You're more than welcome to walk around the hospital. But don't go around doing anything stupid, okay?"

"Thank you very much."

Elrich got up and left the white room. He walked down a marble hallway with purple painted stripes on either side. He walked slowly taking time to look out various windows to see the dark forest lit by large numbers of fireflies. He stopped, turned and faced out one of the windows. Just as a silver skinned necrolyte came walking behind him.

"How's it going Elrich, I heard you had some problems on your mission."

Elrich turned to face this person.

"My teacher, why have you come here in my time of disgrace?

He smiled and then reached into his pocket and pulled out a small vial. It glowed a dark forest green.

"You did everything right, my pupil. You fooled the Matriarch into believing you were me and that I was training an avian. You learned how to draw power without using your soul. You fought enemies of varying levels and you came out on top. You only lost in one direction. You didn't get the girl, but I took the blame in your stead, so you don't have to worry about anything now."

His teacher handed him the vial.

"Here is your soul back, you made me proud kid."

He opened the vial and the vapor floated around into Elrich and the dark forest green color of the vapor appeared in Elrich's eyes. Elrich blinked once, and then again. Tears came streaming from his face. He fell to his knees and put his head in his lap and began to weep.

"I did horrible things teacher, I shouldn't be rewarded."

"You're not my student anymore; you're getting exactly what you deserve. This is not a reward, its what you rightfully earned. Have you ever heard of the ten Contaras?"

Elrich got up and dried his tears and faced his teacher. Not as his teacher but now as his superior in power.

"Yes sir, they're the ten most powerful warriors in our brotherhood with the Avians."

"Yes they're all chosen by others of the Contaras we watch them. Sadly, with the death of the Patriarch, a position became open. Now your pairing with Cassanova was done so that we would test to see if he was ready. They figured a knight would be a perfect candidate. We told this to the Matriarch, though secretly we put you in my place so that we could see if you were ready for the challenge. Personally I knew you were better than that idiot."

Elrich looked at his teacher oddly.

"Yes, Elrich my former pupil, you now belong with us, you're one of the top warriors among the Brotherhood. You are a Contara."

Elrich smiled.

"So what do I have to do?" Elrich asked.

"Hold out your hands and I will recite the chant."

Elrichs teacher took his hand and closed his eyes. There was mumbling of words that seemed to be from an ancient time and then an eight appeared on Elrich's hand.

"The number indicates your strength among the other ten. The more you grow in power the higher your number becomes. And you will have to become more powerful than the current seven to gain the rank of seven."

Elrich looked at his palm.

"Thank you, teacher - but if you don't mind I would like some time to think."

"Sure thing kid, I have to get to my latest pupil, anyway. You know he goes at killing avidly. Not like you - I mean it took so long for you to even accept your gift and learn to embrace the power. But I have to say you have grown to become a harbinger of death now haven't you?"

He walked down the hall turned a corner and vanished. Elrich watched and waited; when he left he ripped his bandages and revealed the huge scar that lined down his chest.

"I am a monster. I used people, hurt people, and I even took Cassanova's soul from his dead body to try and capture some little girl who I had no idea what was so special about anyway. He was a great warrior, a great person. It's a real shame."